We Wish You a Merry Christmas

≫ A TRADITIONAL CHRISTMAS CAROL ≪

pictures by **TRACEY CAMPBELL PEARSON**

Dial Books for Young Readers

E. P. DUTTON, INC.
New York

Published by Dial Books for Young Readers
A Division of E. P. Dutton, Inc.
2 Park Avenue
New York, New York 10016

Library of Congress Cataloging in Publication Data
We wish you a merry Christmas.
Summary: An illustrated version of
the traditional English carol centering
on good cheer and figgy pudding.
1. Christmas music. 2. Carols, English.
3. Folk songs, English. [1. Christmas music.
2. Carols, English. 3. Folk songs, English.]
I. Pearson, Tracey Campbell, ill.
PZ8.3.W37   1983   783.6′5   [E]   82-22224
ISBN 0-8037-9368-5   ISBN 0-8037-9400-2 (lib. bdg.)

Printed in Hong Kong by South China Printing Co.
First Edition
10 9 8 7 6 5 4 3 2 1
The art for each picture consists of an ink, watercolor,
and gouache painting that is camera-separated
and reproduced in full color.

J
783.6
WEW

4/87

For Mom, Dad, and Aunt Nini

We wish you a merry Christmas,

We wish you a merry Christmas,

We wish you a merry Christmas,
And a happy New Year.

Good tidings we bring
To you and your kin.

We wish you a merry Christmas,
And a happy New Year.

Now bring us some figgy pudding,

Now bring us some figgy pudding,

Now bring us some figgy pudding,
And bring some out here.

For we all like figgy pudding,
For we all like figgy pudding,

For we all like figgy pudding,

So bring some out here.

And we won't go till we've got some,
And we won't go till we've got some,
And we won't go till we've got some,

So bring some…

out…here….

We Wish You a Merry Christmas

Traditional Carol from the West Country of England

2.
Now bring us some figgy pudding,
Now bring us some figgy pudding,
Now bring us some figgy pudding,
And bring some out here.
Chorus

3.
For we all like figgy pudding,
For we all like figgy pudding,
For we all like figgy pudding,
So bring some out here.
Chorus

4.
And we won't go till we've got some,
And we won't go till we've got some,
And we won't go till we've got some,
So bring some out here.
Chorus